Venus

and

Seven Reasons I Said No

LIANA BROOKS

OTHER WORKS

HEROES AND VILLAINS

Even Villains Fall In Love
Even Villains Go To The Movies
Even Villains Have Interns
Even Villains Play The Hero (books 1 – 3 omnibus)
The Polar Terror

FLEET OF MALIK

Bodies In Motion
Change of Momentum
For Every Action (forthcoming)

SHORTER WORKS

All I Want For Christmas Is A Werewolf
Darkness and Good
Fey Lights
Prime Sensations

Find other works by the author at
www.lianabrooks.com

Venus

and

Seven Reasons I Said No

INKLET #37

LIANA BROOKS

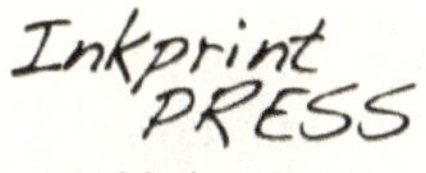

www.inkprintpress.com

Print ISBN: 978-1-925825-30-5
eBook ISBN: 9781393855804

www.inkprintpress.com

National Library of Australia Cataloguing-in-Publication Data
Brooks, Liana 1982 –
Venus and Seven Reasons I Said No (Double Issue)
48 p.
ISBN: 978-1-925825-30-5
Inkprint Press, Canberra, Australia
1. Fiction—Fantasy—Romantic 2. Fiction—Fantasy—Humorous 3. Fiction—Short Stories

First Print Edition: July 2020
Cover design © Inkprint Press
Interior art © Amy Laurens

VENUS

Venus walked through the main door as thunder rolled overhead and the rain began to fall. She glared over her shoulder at the rain then flounced to the front desk of the most expensive hotel in New York City. "Reservation for Vanessa Rome, please." She gave the concierge her best smile. He didn't look dazzled.

He tilted his balding head forward to peer at the computer screen. "I'm sorry, ma'am, we don't have a reservation for anyone by that name."

Venus sighed. "My Daddy made the reservation for me, can you check for Dios Rome, please?" Again she smiled dazzlingly at him.

"I'm sorry, ma'am, but the only reservation we have for that name was last month. My computer shows that no one claimed the room and the card used to reserve it was charged for the full three days. Are you certain you didn't get your travel dates wrong?"

She did a quick mental count. "Blast, what's his name changed the calendars, didn't he?"

"Ma'am?"

"The one with the green shorts," Venus raged, godly powers overflowing. She wiped away a tear of frustration from her eye. "Daddy never remembers the date changes. The two extra months and the New Year starting in the middle of winter rather than when Persephone returns from Hades. It's really too much!"

"Of course." The concierge cleared his throat. "Would you like me to call you a cab, ma'am?"

"A cab?"

"Yes, a cab, we're fully booked this evening. I can't offer you a new reservation."

"You can't?"

"No, ma'am. We're full. You will need to go somewhere else."

Venus's immortal power surged, her eyes narrowed, and she balled her fists, ready to attack her victim.

"Gregory?" A blonde woman pushed past her, rushing to the concierge.

"Marian?" He stared at her in shock. "I haven't seen you... I meant to... I can explain..."

"Oh, Gregory, there's nothing to explain! I understand perfectly and my answer is"—she blushed and looked down—"yes. Yes, I will marry you!"

As the happily reunited couple burst into a frenzy of sweet coos, whispered promises, and lusty kisses, Venus altered the guest book. A few minor changes and the penthouse-with-a-view was hers.

She cleared her throat. "My reservation," she reminded the lipstick-covered man. "I'd like my room key, thank you. Now."

"Yes, of course, right away." He didn't even question how his full hotel suddenly had a penthouse free.

Venus took the room key with a final look of disgust.

"The room will be ready in an hour." The woman trying to give him mouth-to-mouth resuscitation swallowed up the man's line of patter.

"Jupiter almighty!" Venus swung her multi-colored Fendi handbag and stalked back out into the night. The thunder grumbled overhead as the rain subsided. Her gold Gucci heels clicked on the cement as she tried to breathe the fetid city air.

A Mercedes drove past, splashing her shimmering peach dress. Her fists clenched. "How dare you!"

With a graceful flick of her wrist, Venus dried her dress. She tossed her perfect mane of dark hair and crossed with the light.

Immortal wrath churned, reaching out to punish the horrible human.

A horn blared, tires squealed, and the crunch of a black Mercedes hitting a mini-van sounded. Venus looked back with an evil smile.

The woman in the Mercedes jumped out, nearly tripping over a manhole, raging at the driver of the mini-van.

He got out, yelled at her, yelled again in delight when he realized who he was yelling at, and they started kissing.

"Jupiter almighty, you've got to be kidding me!" Venus moaned as the onlookers clapped.

A media-outlets man-on-the-street

cam stopped to interview the happily reunited couple.

"It's so unfair!"

She kept walking, window shopping through the best part of the city, while all around her, smited humans fell in love, rekindled old romances, decided to give love a chance. Her stomach roiled as a feuding couple in a café put differences aside so they could kiss and make-up.

Despondent, Venus slunk into a shabby bookstore and curled up in an over-stuffed armchair to sip a hot cocoa with extra whipped cream.

"Bad day?" the barista asked as she placed a napkin next to Venus on the side table.

"The worst! My reservations at the hotel were messed up, I just had a fight with my husband, and now everywhere I look people are falling in love again. I hate that!"

"Too bad," the girl said carelessly.

"What about you?" Venus asked with a sniffle. "You have some hot body to curl up with tonight?"

"Nope. I prefer cold and dead." The girl slipped her a card before walking away: *Hit Girls: Taking care of problems and cleaning your closet since 1982. First time free.*

Venus turned the card over, thinking. It wasn't that she didn't love Vulcan. It was more that he didn't understand why she was always with Mars.

After all, it was blazingly obvious to everyone but her jealous husband why she was with him. Mars was a wonderful shopping buddy; he always understood why she needed more slingback pumps, he could match colors, and he was madly in love with his hairstylist from Tulsa. Vulcan just didn't understand.

With a snap of her fingers, the card vanished. Hit girls, hit men, hit whatever... That wasn't what she needed.

"David?" The barista was staring at her new customer as if he'd grown a third head.

The Hollywood hero smiled as he pulled a gun. "Sorry, Babes, you know how it is."

"But, we, I..." A coffee mug dropped from her hands, shattering on the ground as the barista backed away.

The man stood.

The ground shook.

The door to the bookstore opened. Lightning cut across the sky, silhouetting a familiar form. He walked in, adjusting glasses that hid his too-green eyes. The well-cut suit he wore accented his well-muscled frame.

Venus sighed. The Romans had it all wrong. She'd definitely married the hottest man on Olympus Mons.

Vulcan sat down across from her. "I'm sorry."

She sat up. Vulcan never said sorry. In their long, tempestuous marriage, she could count the number of apologies he'd given on one hand.

He never *said* sorry, but he showed it in the little things he did. A new vase of black glass, diamonds, a new mountain range in some far-off tropical locale...

"Come on, don't make me say it again."

Venus shook her head and put her mug down with care. "No. You're sorry? Really?"

"I went to surprise you with Mars..." He broke off and blushed.

Venus blushed in sympathy. Vulcan wasn't just near-sighted, sometimes he was downright blind. She cleared her throat. "He's a nice boy, and they make each other happy."

Vulcan turned bright red. "It's just, I expected... Jupiter!" He leaned towards her. "Venus, you're so beautiful I can't imagine how any man would turn you away for, for... anyone else."

Venus studied her nails with interest. There was a story there. If you got upset because the boy you love swung the other way, well, blame it on Hera. Venus knew and was keeping the blackmail tucked away for a rainy day.

"Don't worry about. I never notice them. Just you." She smiled up at Vulcan, batted her eyelashes, took his breath away...

Behind them the world began to move again. David stepped forward, gun still aimed at the betrayed barista's heart. The coffee-girl tilted her chin up defiantly. "Go ahead, you've already broken my heart."

Vulcan looked over and then winked at Venus. "Aren't you going to give the girl a break?"

Venus smiled.

David dropped the gun. "Marry me. We'll run away together. No one ever needs to know..."

SEVEN REASONS I SAID NO: A LIST BY KELLY ANN MORGANSTEIN

1. *It was Nathaniel.*
2. *He stumbled the proposal and my father finished for him.*
3. *Instead of a nice dinner out and a ring, my mother made him dinner at our house and he asked during the salad course. No ring.*
4. *Nathaniel wears yellow socks.*
5. *I'm pretty sure he snores.*
6. *Mallory would murder me if I said yes.*
7. *Nathaniel is dead.*

I MEAN SERIOUSLY??? A ZOMBIE? HOW'S

a nice Jewish girl *supposed* to respond? Sure, I'm his last hope for a nice relationship because every other girl has either turned him down or waived a crucifix at him. I get that. Really. But did he need to *tell* me I was his last choice?

So, you know, not only would he not ask me out if I were the last girl on the planet, he literally wouldn't ask me out unless I was the last girl on the planet who hadn't said no *and* he was dead.

That's just cruel.

And having my parents there? Is it too much to ask for a real proposal? You know, a romantic moonlit walk on the beach...

Or a day at the museum, followed by a luscious dinner.

Something impressive.

Sweet potato latkes are tasty, but they aren't romantic. Not when you help make them and have to wash the dishes afterward. And not when the best compliment of the evening is a dead guy telling you you're very obedient.

Obedient? Gosh, Nathaniel! That's just what every girl wants to hear!

You know. When they're three >.<

Not when they're twenty-four and the only single girl in the whole freakin' town. Single, and living in my parent's attic.

Anne Frank never had it this bad. Right now, I'd welcome a world war.

Anything to keep nosey Mrs. S from dropping by tomorrow for breakfast when she will, I guarantee, casually grab my hand, intending to inspect the rock.

Boy is *she* in for a surprise.

You know what I have instead of a ring? A bracelet. One of Nathaniel's. From the hospital. And his original toe tag. So I could be near him or something? I have no clue. It was creepy. I wanted to set fire to him but my mom grabbed the candles before I could.

Back-stabbing mother! Does she really want a half-rotted corpse as a son-in-law? Is she actually that desperate?

I've got to move out. It's the only logical choice. I need to go find my own place and find someone else to date. Someone who isn't dead.

THE MAKING OF

One of these days—if you are terribly incautious and pick the wrong sort of friends—you are going to run into someone who comes up with what sound like delightful ideas right up until the moment you realize that they were very terrible ideas indeed.

The reason these stories exist is because I'm an extrovert who has trouble saying NO to bubbly personalities with large vocabularies.

I should have realized much earlier in life that short stories were not for me. I should have paid attention the warning signs, like my inability to keep a plot short or my penchant for not caring for short stories at all. I should have listened when my gut instinct was to run away.

But I didn't.

And someone with a large vocabulary, a bubbly personality, and big, brown eyes convinced me that writing a short story every month to a theme was a *wonderful* way to pass the time. I'm certain there's a three-page email in the depths of Amy Laurens' Sent folder where she eloquently explained why I wanted to do this.

Consider this a formal apology for my basic inability to get through even a 300-word story without a corpse or a killer. *Venus* was (maybe?) written for Valentine's Day and *Seven Reasons* was (probably?) written for Halloween.

Or maybe I have it backward.

Either way, here's to love, murder, corpses, and doing things with your best friend simply because they are your best friend.

DOWNLOAD YOUR FREE EBOOK

When you buy a print book from Inkprint Press, we like to say THANK YOU by offering you the ebook for free!

Please head to www.inkprintpress.com/inklets/37/ and the use the coupon 37INK to get your copy of this Inklet in epub AND mobi today!
(Coupon will only work once.)

Read more by Liana Brooks!

FLEET OF MALIK
BODIES IN MOTION
CHAPTER ONE

THE PROBLEM WITH VACATIONS, Selena reflected as she adjusted her sweater outside Cargo Blue, was that reality was always waiting at the end. A quick search of the local security cameras found one that showed the peeling sunburn on her right shoulder blade.

Such was the curse of pale-skinned, ship-born Fleet personnel. Anytime she left the foggy belts covering the city of Tarrin, she barbecued like a shrimp, no matter how much sunscreen she applied. Otherwise, she'd flee even further from the Fleet Enclave and make her home on the equatorial beaches of the planet they were trapped on.

She panned the camera and checked her left shoulder. Black ink made a star-scape that disguised three silver scars as shooting stars. The painting covered her shoulder blade and part of her upper arm. As the artist had promised, the skin-paint had kept her from burning as much, though it still had the over-stretched feel of a burn. With a few adjustments, her uniform covered most of the temporary art; it would keep her from having to explain to her colleagues.

Her forearm warmed, a warning that someone was about to contact her through the tech implant tucked between her radius and ulna.

She hesitated too long and the call came through, a persistent ping against her skull as the phantom image of her best friend floated on the edge of her vision.

Selena turned off the visual receiver and answered. "Genevieve," she said with a smile as the image of her vivacious, red-headed friend appeared floating against the backdrop of landing gear that supported the grounded fleet.

A grounder would have thought she was talking to herself, but grounders wouldn't set foot near the neo-city-state of

Enclave. The rocky beach served as a city and tomb for the survivors of the last war.

"Selena!" Gen gushed. "Starcom to Selena. Where are you? I'm covering for now."

"Delayed, but almost there." Selena hoped Gen wouldn't hear the lie. She'd been standing in the shadows of the Enclave pub for nearly a quarter hour.

"The *Lorenza* could get here faster," Gen said, referencing a long-dead ship whose crew were found skeletonized at their stations. Gen blew hair off her face. "Stars above, you're an hour late. The whole fleet is flying faster than you."

Selena turned on her visual long enough to roll her eyes at her friend. "Ha, ha, funny. That joke needs to be forcibly retired." Sooner rather than later. The fleet couldn't fly without fuel, and the Malik system they were stranded in held precious few deposits of the orun crystals needed to power the ships.

"If you don't come," Gen said threateningly, "I will teleport to your apartment and drag you out in your pajamas."

"I'm not at home," Selena admitted. And she wouldn't have let her best friend come to her new house if she was.

Gen was smart enough to realize that the small palace Selena had bought in downtown Tarrin wasn't paid for by her official OIA salary. The paygrades for the Office of Imperial Affairs had last been updated when the Malik system was still in contact with the empire, making them 900 years out of date.

Technically, taking a second job wasn't treason, but there were enough people in the fleet who'd see it as a betrayal that keeping it secret felt right. Especially since Gen's captain was one who would scream the loudest.

Gen clapped. "Selena! Stop stalling yer engines and get in here. This isn't some Fleet Tribunal, just our friends. You, me, Carver. I left a message for Marshall. You know. People we like."

The light of understanding dawned. "Carver? This is so you can snuggle up to Perrin Carver without your parents watching?"

"Yes," Gen admitted, not looking the least bit contrite.

"You're only dragging me along so I can cover for you while you make out in a corner, aren't you?" She masked the relief with mock anger. At least Gen wasn't trying to set Selena up with one of her cousins. Or, ancestors forbid, Gen's handsy older brother.

Again.

Gen opened her eyes wide with an innocent smile. "Maybe."

"Gen!" Selena rolled her eyes. "Doesn't he have his own place?"

"Just the bachelor's dorm. The Carvers didn't have any ships except the shuttle his parents crashed in. Making out next door to Mom and Dad? No. And the BOQ? It's so tacky. You can hear everything through those walls."

Selena hid a smile. "I'll be there soon enough."

If Gen ever caught wind of how panicky the thought of a relationship made her, Gen would make it her life's goal to see Selena paired off. And there wasn't a man alive who she could imagine getting close to now.

Her implant helpfully pulled up an image of a tall, broad-shouldered, lean-muscled fighter with skin black as the night between stars and emerald-green eyes.

She pushed the memory away.

Lieutenant Commander Titan Sciarra was striking, intelligent, and had a body she'd cross battle lines for, but he was also out of reach. There was no point in chasing a man who wouldn't give her the time of day.

Another crew shuffled past her into the bar, black patches with silver fists on their shoulders.

It was getting harder to pretend she belonged in Enclave, with the fleet. Once upon a time, she'd known every crew's patch without thinking. She could name captains, their ships and their seconds by rote.

Now she would need to tap into the fleet's information nexus if she wanted to know who they were.

She stopped at the edge of the door to tug her lightest shields into place. A few minor adjustments would keep bugs away, keep beer off her clothes, and prevent anyone from hacking into her implant. They could still send messages, because disallowing that would have raised eyebrows. And they could still hit her. But she could always hit back.

Selena rolled her shoulders and strutted into Cargo Blue. It was a battle-field, but she was the last captain of the Caryll family, and she wasn't going down without a fight.

Whatever crew owned Cargo Blue probably hadn't had much of a decorating budget, but at least they'd stuck with a theme: oversized cargo boxes were piled up to make walls, seating, and tables. Olive-green safety webbing draped from the ceiling between blue lights. Fog used for fire drills on the ships pumped across the floor to hide the concrete beneath.

There was no bouncer at the door, but people were still hanging around the entrance.

As a rule, the fleet was cautious, and the young faces she saw belonged to fleet members who had never ventured outside their own crew more than a few times, even though the fleet had been grounded for nearly three years.

Tables to the left, bar ahead, dance floor to the right... and that meant the back half of the cargo hanger had been partitioned and karaoke would be in the back right corner. After a few minutes of weaving through the human crush, she found Gen, already sitting in Perrin Carver's lap and giggling.

"Selena!" Gen jumped up and hugged her. "I was beginning to worry!"

"How many people are in here?" Selena shouted over the music.

"Everyone under forty?" Gen laughed. With a small hand wave Gen put up a minor sound shield, muting the music. "People are going to stir crazy. Combine that with the anniversary—"

The anniversary.

Today.

The day the war had begun, the day the

united fleet had died.

They'd been dying for four hundred years, well aware that the reserve of orun crystals was depleted and there was no way to move forward with the ships they had.

Old Captain Baular had seen the deposit of orun on the fifth planet as their saving grace. He'd get it even if it meant killing the grounders.

And, coward that he was, he'd ordered his grandson to lead the first attack instead of leading it himself.

That opening skirmish began and ended in the dark, with Titan Sciarra in the infirmary, and five Academy fighters mis-sing or damaged. But by lunch of the next day, every officer belonging to crews allied with the Baulars withdrew.

Seven months later, heated words turned to live rounds.

"Selena?" Gen asked quietly, placing a hand on her arm. "You didn't know the date, did you?"

"I was trying not to think about." If she had, she'd have cut her vacation to the islands early. Maybe even made her pilgrimage to the small cay where she'd ditched her stolen fighter after driving off the attack.

She rolled her shoulder, stretching the deep scars. "It snuck up on me."

"First round, we drink to the Lost Fleet, and all who've gone on to crew it. I'm buying," Gen said with a touch of forced joviality. "Carver's been making friends. Tell her, babe." She pushed Carver's shoulder.

Perrin Carver was tall, broad-shouldered man with shy, hazel eyes that hid a wicked sense of humor.

Selena's heart fluttered just a little at the memory of a time when she'd fancied herself in love with him. He'd been the ideal starsider: intelligent, good-looking, and charismatic. They'd been friends of a sort, but even that relationship had soured when she'd realized he'd been getting close to her so he could learn more about Genevieve Silar.

Carver nodded and held out his hand. "Hi, Selena. How are you?"

She tapped the back of his hand with hers, letting him test her shields. "Good. How's the Starguard?"

"Booming." The commander of the Starguard smiled, white teeth flashing, but there was a tightness around his eyes. "Everyone hears about guardians being allowed outside the Enclave, or working with the Jhandarmi, and I'm drowning in recruiting requests. Captains of larger crews invite me to Captain's Mess so they can introduce me to their best and brightest. Half the time I can't tell if they want me to marry into the crew or take the fleetlings into the guard." His shield was still attached to hers, scanning her as he talked.

All he would get from her was polite interest. Her heartrate didn't spike or dip at the mention of the Jhandarmi. Her smile never flickered.

"Maybe you should lock down Gen," Selena said. "If you had a spouse, no one would try to get you to marry into the crew."

Carver and Gen shared a look, and Gen

sent a ping of information that Selena's implant translated as an ongoing debate over crew name and a place to live.

Carver sent something similar; a picture of his bachelor's quarters and his one ship.

There was no room for them to marry and have a family.

"Enclave is a temporary solution," Selena said out loud. She'd lost the taste for communicating by implant years ago. "If we—"

A heavy hand wrapped around her waist as someone wearing too much cologne stepped far too close to her. "Hello, Selena."

Hollis Silar, one of Gen's many siblings, kissed her temple.

Simultaneously, Selena sighed, sent a shock through her shield to Hollis's hand, and elbowed him in the gut. "Hi, Hollis. I see you're still bathing in cologne rather than water."

He stepped away from her, an easy smile still in place.

It wasn't that Hollis was bad looking;

plenty of women found him handsome.

It was that he was equally affectionate with every woman he saw and he couldn't keep a secret to save his life. Or anyone else's.

He'd chase anyone with a pretty smile and fell in and out of love a couple of times a day.

"Nice to see you too, Selena. Now, everyone, you're all going to look at me, smile, and laugh like I'm my normal, dashing self," he said, his smile never changing. "You haven't been paying attention, but I'm not a member of the Starguard for nothing. We're being watched. Now take your nice drinks from the waitress and keep your eyes on me."

Hollis nodded to the waitress and handed out four cups with bright purple liquid. "Bruised Stars all around. Guaranteed to make you giggle, or so the guy at the bar told me. Although he's a Seutaai, so take it with a shield in place." He handed Selena her drink with a smile, but turned immediately to glance over his shoulder.

"Big brother, who are we looking for?" Gen asked with a slow drawl. "Is it a friend who you might have forgotten to call back after a night out?"

Hollis shook his head. "No, I thought I saw some of the Lee crew. Make that, I'm certain of it."

Selena grimaced. "As long as Rowena isn't here."

"Did you call me?"

Startled, Selena looked up to the face of her least favorite woman: Rowena Lee.

"Hello," Selena said politely. "I see you're still alive. That's…"

Unfortunate.

She nodded and took a slug of her Bruised Star.

Rowena held up a tray of electric blue shots. "My crew thinks I can't out-drink anyone in this bar. I probably can't go toe-to-toe with alcoholics like the Silars here. But No-Shot Selena?" Rowena set the drinks on the table. "I can out-shoot you in the stars or on the ground."

Gen sucked in air between her teeth and sent Selena several urgent pings telling her to ignore the Lees.

Selena muted Gen. "I took plenty of shots in the war. As I recall, I disabled three of your big birds. *Bassi, Aryton, Theoano...* Bang, bang, bang." Selena mimed firing with her finger. "Three shots. Three silent ships."

"Not kills," Rowena said. "A whole war and you never blooded yourself."

That was it, the memory she didn't want to face; the time she'd almost taken Death's claim and risked killing someone outside of war.

"That's uncalled for," Hollis said, trying to step between them. "Selena, why don't we—"

Selena pushed Hollis aside and grabbed the first shot.

She tossed back the potent drink and shattered the glass on the table. "Go suck vacuum, Rowena. You're a pissant yeoman with no hope of command."

"I went to the Academy, same as you, Selena. I fought for the fleet." Rowena slammed a shot back. "You fought for the mud-lickers."

Selena took another shot as the first started to fuzz her judgement. "I prevented the Baulars from committing mass genocide and destroying the civilians along with the fleet."

Rowena took her second shot. A crowd was gathering and that seemed to feed her cruelty. "The Lees survived the war. We're still here. How many Caryll captains are there? Oh, right, one. Can you count that high, No-Shot? You have any idea how easy it would be for me to end you right now?"

Selena took the last two glasses and slammed them both back.

Gen pinged her, giving locations, counts, and identities of the Lee allies in the crowd.

Hollis stepped to her flank, ready to defend her.

She stood, anger burning through her veins. "Sure, your crew outnumbers mine. I guess on paper, it's not really a fair fight, is it, Rowena? But you were trained as a flight leader, and what do Carylls do? Hand-to-hand combat. Maybe I should thin your ranks, starting with one mouthy yeoman."

Keep reading! Head to:
<u>www.inkprintpress.com/ liana-brooks/fleet-of-malik/bodies-in-motion/</u>

ABOUT THE AUTHOR

Despite her use of archaic languages and a frightening understanding of Latin, Liana says she isn't an undying immortal or goddess of any kind. We think it's best to take her word for it; after all, if she *is* an immortal goddess we wouldn't want to make her angry.

When she isn't meddling with the affairs of mortals, Liana enjoys writing space opera (*Fleet of Malik*) and super villain romances (*Heroes and Villains*).

You can learn more about her and her books at www.LianaBrooks.com.

INKLET #031
Welcome to Dark Dale
LIANA BROOKS

INKLET #032
When War Came to Town
A Powers Story
AMY LAURENS

INKLET #033
Not Fantasy
AMY LAURENS

INKLET #034
Courting the Winter Prince
LIANA BROOKS

INKLET #035
At the Home of the Winter King
A Seven Gates Story
AMY LAURENS

INKLET #036
With This Ring
AMY LAURENS

INKLET #037
Venus & Seven Reasons I Said No
LIANA BROOKS

INKLET #038
OATH KEEPER
AMY LAURENS

INKLET #035
FORGET
A Powers Story
AMY LAURENS

INKLET #040
NOT QUITE Cinderella
LIANA BROOKS

INKLET #041
ONE BAD MAN
AMY LAURENS

DOUBLE ISSUE
INKLET #042
The Claustrophobia Of Loneliness &
Adam, Be A Star
AMY LAURENS

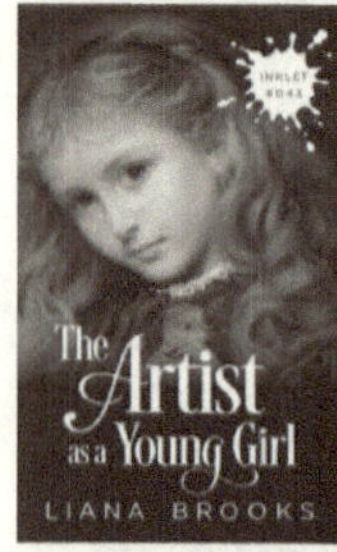

INKLET #043
The Artist as a Young Girl
LIANA BROOKS

INKLET #044
CONFESSIONS
AMY LAURENS

INKLET #045
But For Snow
A Kaditeos Story
AMY LAURENS

INKLET #046
The Boy Named NO
LIANA BROOKS

INKLET #047
Anamata
AMY LAURENS

INKLET #048
A Wolf FOR Christmas
AMY LAURENS